Other Books by Lois Lenski

FLOOD FRIDAY

FLOOD FRIDAY

LOIS LENSKI

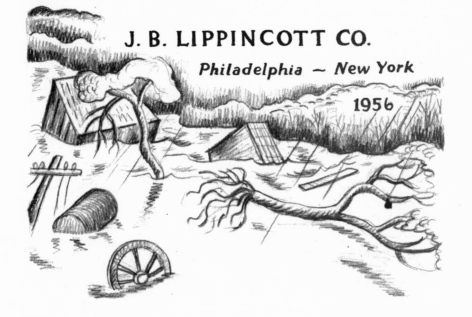

J. B. LIPPINCOTT CO.
Philadelphia ~ New York

1956

Copyright ©, 1956, by Lois Lenski

Lithographed in the United States of America

Fifth Printing

Library of Congress Catalog Card Number 56-9901

Nil.

To
all the flood children
with love

FOREWORD

"Our house went."

"A knock came at the door. I was so scared, I was shaking."

"I saw the neighbor kids in the water, going down and coming back up."

"My mother felt bad. She lost her big Bible."

"I never saw our house after it went, but my father did. The water took it away at nine in the morning. It went floating down the street. The nails fell out and it broke in pieces."

Such words from the lips of children convey the full meaning of the flood tragedy, which struck Connecticut on Flood Friday, August 19, 1955. Such words, too, convey their innate stoicism and courage, their acceptance of the inevitable, and their resilience in the face of danger.

Thousands of children in the United States have lived through major floods in the last decade. Not only those in Connecticut and adjoining states, but along the Ohio, Mississippi and Missouri rivers, and in California and Texas, children know what floods mean. This book is for them, and for all those more fortunate children who can share their experiences only through books.

In October after the flood, a little girl in Ohio wrote me:

"I have an idea for a book of yours. It would be about the horrible flood! How one family was rescued and what happened to them or if they were hurt."

I am grateful to her, and to the children of Union School, Unionville, Connecticut, who invited me to come to write of their experiences. Living in the heart of the flooded area of Connecticut, I felt a compelling urge to write this book.

Lois Lenski

BAD OLD RIVER

Words by Lois Lenski
Music by Clyde Robert Bulla

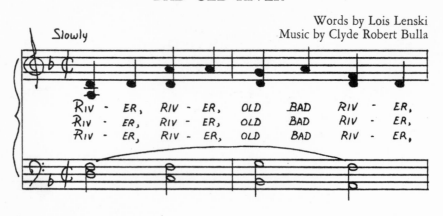

Slowly

Riv - er, Riv - er, old bad Riv - er,
Riv - er, Riv - er, old bad Riv - er,
Riv - er, Riv - er, old bad Riv - er,

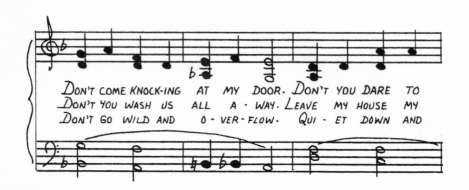

Don't come knock-ing at my door. Don't you dare to
Don't you wash us all a - way. Leave my house my
Don't go wild and o - ver-flow. Qui - et down and

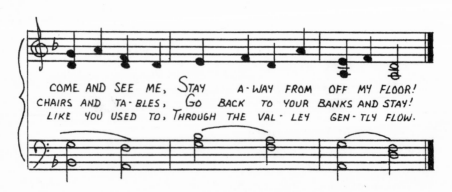

come and see me, Stay a - way from off my floor!
chairs and ta - bles, Go back to your banks and stay!
like you used to, Through the val - ley gen - tly flow.

CONTENTS

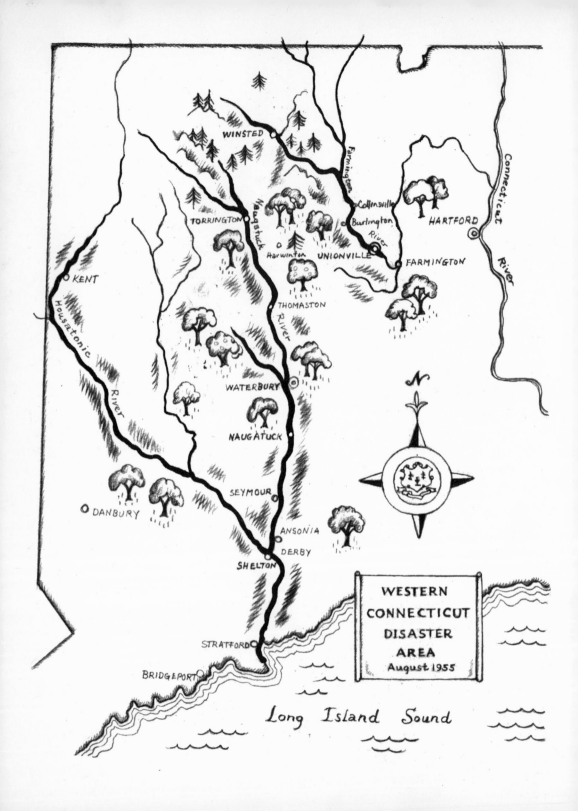

WESTERN
CONNECTICUT
DISASTER
AREA
August 1955

Long Island Sound

FLOOD FRIDAY

1

RISING WATER

I'm having chocolate nut," said Barbara Boyd.

"I'll take strawberry," said Sally Graham.

"Vanilla for me," said Sally's sister Karen.

The three girls were perched up on stools at the soda counter. They began to sip their ice cream. Sally watched the people coming in.

The little River Bend store was crowded. It was Thursday, a hot, muggy day in August. Outside it was raining hard. The children wore raincoats and rubbers. Everybody who came in was

3

dripping. Cars stopped outside and people picked up groceries. Children came in on errands or to get ice cream.

"Look who's coming!" cried Sally.

Carol Rosansky and David Joruska came in.

"Hi, Carol!" called Sally.

"Hi, David!" said Barbara.

Carol and David got up on stools and ordered cold drinks. Then Angela Marciano, who was thirteen, came in bringing her five-year-old sister Linda. Her brothers, Tony and Al, followed, with Tommy Dillon. Ray and Ralph Marberry came too. They all lived in River Bend.

"Gee! Our whole school will soon be here," said Sally.

"When it rains like this," said David, "there's no place to go to but the store. It's dry in here."

The Marcianos and Tommy Dillon crowded up close behind the girls.

"Our back yard is full of water," said Angela Marciano. "I never saw so much water in the river before."

"Aw! That's nothing," said Tommy Dillon. "It's fine weather for ducks. Go take a swim!"

Tommy Dillon was a small, thin boy of eleven, one of a family of seven children. His house was not far from the Grahams. At school the year before, he had sat behind Sally Graham and made her life miserable.

Now he pushed and shoved behind her, reaching for his bottle of soda. He tipped it up and drank.

Sally opened her purse and took out her new compact. It was shiny like gold and had a blue enameled bird on the cover. It was just new. She had bought it the previous Saturday at the dime store in Hartford. She snapped it open, looked at herself, took out the powder puff and powdered her nose. In the mirror, she saw Tommy Dillon behind her, grinning.

"That's right! Powder your nose!" cried Tommy. "Did you bring your lipstick too?"

The next moment Tommy snatched the compact out of Sally's hand. It disappeared in his pocket. Sally turned on him angrily.

"Did you lose something?" asked Tommy innocently.

"You give my compact right back, Tommy Dillon!" cried Sally.

Tommy set his empty bottle on the counter and tossed a coin to the clerk. Then he made for the door. Sally and Barbara had to pay for their ice cream. The Marciano children took their places on the stools.

"Beat it, Tommy!" shouted the Marberry boys.

"Get going, Tommy!" yelled Tony and Al Marciano.

"Oh, Sally!" cried Angela. "Make him give it back."

The girls dashed out in the rain after Tommy Dillon and the store door banged behind them.

"You'll never catch him, Sally," said Barbara.

"I've got to," cried Sally. "He took my new compact!"

It was raining harder than ever now. Cars passed both ways on the highway, splashing water as they went. Before they knew it, Tommy had darted across. The girls had to wait for a lull in the traffic. When they reached the other side, Tommy was nowhere in sight.

"That mean old Tommy Dillon!" cried Sally. She was so angry she was ready to cry. "He's mean. I hate him."

"Can't you get another compact?" asked Karen.

"Of course not," said Sally. "I spent my whole week's allowance on that one. And it was the only one they had with a bluebird on it."

"Oh, what do you care?" said Barbara Boyd. "Who wants a compact, anyhow?"

"I do," said Sally.

Barbara Boyd was Sally Graham's best friend, but sometimes Sally found it hard to understand her. Barbara never powdered her nose at all, and she never painted her nails.

"Well, Mother told you not to buy it," said Karen.

"She just said I was too young," said Sally.

The girls left the highway and walked down a side street of River Bend toward their homes. Barbara's brothers, Dan and Ronnie, came out of the Boyd house.

"Where are you boys going?" asked Barbara.

"Down to see the river," said Dan.

"The river?" said Sally. "What for? Going for a swim?"

"The river's rising," said Dan. "There's going to be a flood. We heard it over the radio."

"We've got the river right in our back yard," said Sally. "Let's go to my house and look at it."

The boys followed the girls down several blocks toward the river, where the Graham house was located. They went around to the back yard.

"The river looks just the same as always," said Sally.

"No," said Karen, pointing. "It's up as far as the apple tree. Look! The river's coming to see us."

The children laughed.

"Where's the doghouse?" asked Sally suddenly.

The children looked around. The river was wider than they had ever seen it before.

"There goes the doghouse! It's floating," said Dan Boyd.

"That's not it," said Sally, worried. "That looks like a barrel."

"Look at all the things floating," said Barbara. "I never saw things come down the river like this before."

"There goes a tree . . ."

"And cartons and a wagon wheel . . ."

"And look! Somebody's chair is floating!"

The children were excited now, pointing and laughing.

"Where's Rusty's doghouse?" asked Sally again. All she could think of was the dog.

"It's gone," said Karen. "I bet the river's carried it off."

Sally looked around and saw her mother coming out of the back door.

"Mother," she called. "Is Rusty in the house?"

"Yes," said Mrs. Graham. "He's playing with Jack and Tim."

"His doghouse is gone," said Karen. "Good thing Rusty wasn't inside."

"I used the wheelbarrow and moved the doghouse up on the porch," said Mrs. Graham. "Come and help me, children. Let's bring the table and chairs in."

Dan and Ronnie and the girls helped. Soon the lawn furniture was safely under the porch roof, beside the doghouse and Bobby's and Sally's bicycles. Mrs. Graham sat down on a chair and took off her shoes and stockings.

"What are you going to do, Mother?" asked Sally.

"Pick my zinnias," said Mrs. Graham.

"The flower bed is a pond now!" said Barbara Boyd.

"Well, I'll wade in," said Mrs. Graham. "If it's never going to stop raining, I'd like to have a bouquet in the house to cheer us up."

The children laughed. They watched Mrs. Graham wade in the water and come out with a bunch of flowers. The Boyd children said goodbye and went on home.

"See you tomorrow!" Barbara called back.

"Sure!" answered Sally. Little did she realize what was to happen before she saw her best friend again.

"Rusty! Rusty!" she called as she went inside.

The little long-haired dog jumped up on her as she came in the door. She picked him up and gave him a hug.

Sally was restless all evening. She saw neighbors passing by, watching the river. They shook their heads, looking at the heavy sky. Perry Wilson, a next-door neighbor, stopped in to talk with Mother. Sally wished her father would come home.

When he came, Mr. Graham said that several small bridges were washed out, and he had had to make a detour from Hartford. After supper, Sally read a book to Karen, tried to keep the little boys from fighting and gave baby Betty her bottle. Bobby, who was nine, read comics all evening. At last it was time to go to bed. The children trooped up the stairs.

Karen fell asleep quickly. After all, she was only seven. Sally was the oldest, eleven. She kept thinking she heard voices downstairs. Each time she started to fall asleep, they woke her up. Was it the Wilsons again? Why didn't they go home and go to bed?

Once she heard Daddy say, "The cellar's full already. Why was that outside cellar door left open?"

She could not hear Mother's reply. Daddy went on, "We can take the motor upstairs. The sewing machine too. If it comes in here, we'll just carry everything upstairs."

Sally felt comforted and reassured. She knew Daddy and Mother would take care of everything. She fell asleep.

A loud knock came at the door.

Sally woke up suddenly. She was so scared, she was trembling. She knew it was the middle of the night, for she had been asleep a long time. She threw back the quilt and swung quietly out of bed, so as not to wake up Karen. As she was feeling for her slippers, she heard voices outside. She tried to listen.

The windows were open—the night was hot and close. It was still raining hard. But above the sound of the pelting rain, she could hear voices. She looked out the window. She saw people with umbrellas standing in the rain and talking. A policeman was at the door.

"You'll have to get out!" he shouted. "The river is rising."

Sally could not hear what her father answered.

"It's coming up fast," the policeman said. "Don't try to take anything. Get out while you can."

The door banged and he was gone. He was on his way to warn the other River Bend people—the Boyds, the Dillons, the Marcianos and many others.

Sally ran to the head of the stairs. She looked down and was

never to forget what she saw. There, in the place where the floor had been, was water. River water. She stared. Daddy and Mother were wading in it with their feet and legs bare. They were moving things—putting things up higher.

"Mother!" called Sally. *"Mother!"*

"Are you up, Sally?" answered Mother. "Waken the children and help them get dressed."

"Why, Mother," said Sally, *"it's the middle of the night!"*

"Remember when we drove to Maine?" said Mother. "Remember how we started in the middle of the night?"

Sally woke Karen and tried to get some clothes on Bobby and the little boys. Karen took baby Betty and gave her a bottle. Before the children had their shoes on, Mother brought food upstairs—milk, butter and bread. She put it in a basket.

"What's the food for?" asked Sally.

"In case somebody needs it," said Mother. Even at a time like this, Mother was thinking of other people.

The boys saw the water downstairs and thought it a joke.

"There goes the pancake flour!" cried Jack.

"There goes the breadbox!" shouted Tim.

"And I see Daddy's slippers," said Bobby. "They're floating like boats."

Suddenly the lights went out. The electricity had gone off.

"We need cat eyes to see in the dark," said the boys.

Sally looked out the window. It was getting a little lighter outside. She saw things floating by on the great sea of water. Was everything going to be washed away? She kept her eyes on the little pine tree in the yard, the tree Daddy always put the electric lights on at Christmas time. She could only see the tip of it. As she watched, the water came up until even the tip was gone.

Loud bumps could be heard downstairs. Things were banging around. Sally wondered what time it was, but the electric clock had stopped when the lights went out. She heard a bell ringing.

"That's the phone," said Daddy downstairs. "Ringing under water. Somebody's trying to call us."

"Uncle Paul from Burlington, I expect," said Mother. "He'll be worried about us."

Then the town siren went off, long and loud. The children put their hands over their ears.

"That's the signal for everybody," called Daddy. "We must go. We'll have to wade to the car. I left it at the end of the driveway where it's higher."

"But the water!" Mother looked out the upstairs window. "It will be up to our waists, it's rising so fast."

Daddy looked up the stairs. He was standing in the water below. The downstairs rooms were already half full.

"We can make it," said Daddy. "We'll carry the children on our backs."

Suddenly a man's voice called out, "Quick! Get out of your house, Graham. There's no time to lose."

"We're coming!" shouted Daddy. He called to Mother, "Al Barker and some of the firemen are out there. They've come to help us."

"Just in time," said Mother.

"Come to the upstairs window over the porch," Barker shouted. "We've got a boat."

"Thank God," said Mother softly. "Grab your clothes, children."

Karen picked up one of Bobby's coats, tied a scarf round her head, and picked her big rag doll up out of its bed. Sally put on an old jacket of her mothers and her father's old hat. The little boys couldn't find their shoes. It happened so quickly in the dark.

The next minute Daddy was upstairs.

"Quick," he said to Mother. "I'll go first. You hand the kids out to me."

He picked up the baby and crawled out the window onto the porch roof. It was all so sudden, the children made no sound. Taking what lay nearest at hand, they climbed out the window one by one, with Mother's help. They slid across the roof into Daddy's arms. First the little boys, then Karen with her rag doll and Sally. Then a suitcase of clothes and the basket of food. Mother came last. Al Barker helped them down. The next minute they were all sitting in a boat—all but Bobby.

"Bobby, come *on*!" called Mother. "What *are* you doing?"

Bobby crawled out the window, with a piece of cardboard in his hand. He slid to the edge of the porch roof, leaned over and pinned the card to the porch post. Then he jumped into the boat.

The card had words printed on it in black crayon. In the dim light, Daddy read it aloud and laughed. " 'NOBODY HOME BUT WE'LL BE BACK.' That's the right spirit, son."

"Oh, we forgot Rusty!" cried Sally. "He's asleep under my bed."

Daddy whistled and called. The dog heard, jumped on the window sill and barked. Daddy crawled up and brought him

LOIS LENSKI

over. Rusty tumbled into Sally's lap. All the children patted him. They could not leave old Rusty behind.

Fred Joruska, another volunteer fireman, had lashed a rope around the trunk of the elm tree to anchor the boat by the porch. The wind was blowing, making rough waves, and it was still raining hard. Fred released the rope and took up the oars. Al Barker tried to start the outboard motor, but it was wet and would not spark. Mr. Graham helped Joruska with the oars. Bouncing over the rough water, the boat carried the Graham family to safety.

"I never saw such a big river before," said Jack.

"Where are we going?" asked Tim. "To Maine?"

"Hush!" said Mother. The baby began to cry and Mother held her close.

Soon the boat pulled up on a rise of dry land. Everybody got out. They looked around bewildered. It was still raining hard.

"Where are we?" asked Sally.

There was a house on a small hill. Sally knew it at once. It was the Boyds' house. It was where Barbara, her girl-friend, lived.

2

AIR RESCUE

The Boyds' house was dark.

"They're not awake," said Mrs. Graham. "It must be very early."

"They're lucky to live on a hill," said Mr. Graham.

"Where we going, Daddy?" asked Tim. "To Maine?"

"If we had our car," said Mother, "we could go to Uncle Paul's in Burlington."

"We should have started an hour ago," said Daddy, "instead of moving that furniture. Then we could have had the car. Now it's full of water."

17

"Couldn't we go in the Boyds' house?" asked Sally. "They'd let us."

"There's no light," said Mother. "They must be gone. We couldn't go in anyway. We're soaking wet."

The men in the boat called to Mr. Graham and he hurried over. Mrs. Graham stood waiting, the baby in her arms and the children huddled around her. Bobby held Rusty in his arms. Daddy came back.

"They need me to help," he said. "We're going to see about the Dillons and the Marcianos and the Meyers and all those people. It's low there—they are all under water. They were warned in time, but we are not sure they're all out. Will you . . ."

"We'll be all right," said Mother. "Go and help them. Don't worry about us."

"Try and get a ride to Uncle Paul's," said Daddy.

"We will," said Mother. "Somebody will take us, I'm sure."

The men had started the motor now. Mr. Graham got in the boat and they rode off. A block below the Boyd house, in a hollow, stood the Dillon house. It was surrounded by water. The motorboat passed beyond to houses lower down.

Sally held her little brothers by the hand. She kept looking at Mother to see what she would do. Karen and Bobby held to Mother's arms, half asleep.

A car came up and a strange man got out. He wore a Civil Defense helmet. He went to the Boyds' door and knocked loudly.

"Get out!" he called. "The river's rising." There was no answer.

He came over to Mrs. Graham and she told him her story.

"You're lucky to get out," he said.

"Could somebody drive us to my brother's in Burlington?" asked Mrs. Graham.

"No cars available," said the man. "Too many bridges out. Better not try it. If you have friends up in the hills, go to them. Plenty of people are sleeping in their cars up in the hills."

"Our car—it was under water," said Mrs. Graham. "We left it standing in the driveway."

"It's down the river by now," said the man. "They're taking in refugees at Union School. Can't you walk? It's not too far." He knocked at the Boyds' door again.

A light flickered inside. The door opened and there stood Mrs. Boyd. She was up and dressed after all. Barbara stood beside her. The man repeated his warning. He told the Boyds to get out.

"Oh, but we're on high land," said Mrs. Boyd.

"We're warning everybody," said the man. "Stay at your own risk."

"Are the Dillons out?" asked Mrs. Boyd, pointing to their house.

"They can't get to them," said the man. "The current is too swift. Their house is going to go. They were stubborn and waited too long."

"Oh, that poor woman," said Mrs. Boyd, "and all those children, sick with the flu. There are seven of them. They'll be drowned. Can't I help get them out?"

"You can't do a thing," said the man. "You'd better get out yourself. Go while you can in your car. The river will be up here in half an hour, if that dam up north breaks through. The whole Bend will be flooded."

Mrs. Boyd looked at the man.

"We'll go," she said, "but not till the Dillons are out."

The man turned his back. He hurried to the houses beyond.

"Hi, Barbara!" called Sally. "Hi, Barbara!"

Mrs. Boyd had not noticed the Grahams before. She turned to look at the little family group.

"Is that you, Carrie?" she called. "Why didn't you come in? Did you get out all right?"

"We're wet to the skin," said Mrs. Graham. She told of their narrow escape.

"Oh, I'm so glad you made it," said Mrs. Boyd. "Come in and get dry. I'll fix breakfast."

Sally helped Barbara set food out and soon they were eating. It was good to be with Barbara again. Mrs. Graham put the baby and the little boys down on a bed, and soon they were fast asleep. Karen and Bobby fell asleep, too, and even the dog, Rusty.

"I was awake all night," said Mrs. Boyd, "waiting for Jim to come home. He's been out since noon yesterday. I guess I fell asleep on the couch. I didn't see you folks out there at all."

"It's good you live on a hill," said Mrs. Graham.

"I don't think the river will come up this far," said Mrs. Boyd. "Most of the River Bend houses are so low. They should never have been built in that hollow at all. They were flooded in 1936 and now again."

"I remember," said Mrs. Graham. "They were just summer cabins at first."

It was morning now, but not much brighter, for the sky was heavy with black clouds and it was still raining hard. Mrs. Boyd said she would be afraid to drive the Grahams to Burlington, because the radio had reported so many bridges out. Then, too, she did not want to leave until the Dillons were rescued.

Barbara listened, while the women washed dishes and talked. Then she saw Dan and Ronnie Boyd run out the door.

"Let's go with them, Barbara," said Sally. The girls followed.

"There goes a boat," said Dan. "Let's go see them rescue people."

"It's going to the Dillon house," said Barbara. "They must be still inside."

"Maybe the house will wash away," said Ronnie.

Sally's heart skipped a beat. What had happened to their own house since they left it? Could a house really be washed away?

The children went down to the water's edge and watched. The old river banks could no longer be seen. The river was like a great wide lake. Three rows of houses in the lower Bend were half-covered with water. The river was rushing madly downstream. Uprooted trees were floating, also boxes and trash and lumber. Over by the Dillon house, the current was strong.

Two houses came floating down the river. They smacked into each other and one of them broke in half. The broken half hit a floating tree and part of it went under.

The boys laughed. "Look at old Half-and-Half!" they cried.

Sally held to Barbara's arm.

"It's somebody's house," she whispered. "It's somebody's house."

"Maybe they got out like you did," said Barbara.

The children watched in silence. A strange-looking airplane appeared in the sky. It had two whirling propellers on top. The children had never seen one like it before.

"Gee!" cried Ronnie, who was only seven. "It looks like a giant eggbeater!" The girls laughed.

Only Dan knew what it was. "A helicopter!" he said.

"It's coming right over the Dillons' house," said Barbara.

"I see somebody at the upstairs window," said Sally. "Maybe it's Tommy—or Mike."

Sally began to tremble. She had stood at an upstairs window herself. She knew what it was to watch the water come up higher and higher. Now the same thing was happening to Tommy Dillon, whom she hated. Why didn't Al Barker and Fred Joruska come in their boat and take *them* out, too?

The helicopter, a small one, hovered over the flooded houses. The man in it did not seem to see a small figure waving a white towel at the window of the Dillon home. Soon the machine disappeared in the murky, cloudy sky.

"I thought helicopters were supposed to rescue people," said Dan in disgust. "But this one never did a thing."

"The Dillons will just have to swim out," said Ronnie. "Only Mike—he don't know how. He's afraid to even get his toes wet."

Sally remembered all the mean things Tommy Dillon had done to her. But now he was in trouble. How could she go on hating him? Still—he'd better give that compact back, or else . . . There was Mike, too, just Karen's age. The older girl, Mary, had just come home from the hospital, and Helen was in High School. Besides, there were the little ones. What if their house got washed away, with all of them inside?

The children watched in silence. Then they heard a put-put-put sound. A motorboat appeared. Two men were in it, one a policeman. The motor sputtered and died, and the men could not start it again. The boat bounced up and down on the waves. The men tried to row it, but the current was swift. They could not make any headway. It tipped over twice and they righted it, then climbed back in.

"They are trying to get to the Dillons," said Barbara.

Several cars drove up and people got out. They stood and watched, too. Among them was a River Bend neighbor, Mrs. Toska and her daughter Annabelle.

"Whose house is that?" asked Mrs. Toska.

"The Dillons'," said Sally.

"Are they in it?" asked Mrs. Toska.

"Yes," said Barbara. "They're all sick with the flu. That's why they didn't get out earlier."

"Tommy's not sick," said Sally. "He was well enough to swipe my compact yesterday."

"Too bad they didn't go sooner," said Mrs. Toska. "I heard the Webbs' house went. I hope they got out in time."

"There won't be a single house left in River Bend," said Annabelle.

The boat could not get near the Dillon house. The men had beached it now on an isolated rise of land near by. One of the men started casting with a fishing rod. Now Mr. Dillon, who could be seen at the upstairs window, caught the line. A rope was tied to the other end and Mr. Dillon pulled it in. The men shouted back and forth. They tied their end of the rope to a tree on the hill.

"That's to keep the house from going," said Mrs. Toska.

The men on the little island got in the boat again. They rowed over to the road and got out. The Civil Defense man came up in his car and they got in with him. They all drove off.

"Well, I like that!" cried Dan in disgust.

"Are they going away and leave them?" cried Sally. "Why don't they help?" Though she hated Tommy, she desperately wanted him to be saved.

"What can they do?" said Barbara.

"They must be going to radio for help," said Mrs. Toska.

"The house is starting to move," said Dan.

"The rope will hold it," said Barbara.

"Help! Help!" Mr. Dillon called from his window. Behind him, the white faces of his wife and children could be seen.

Sally hid her face in her hands. She could not look any more. Just then, a whirring, buzzing sound was heard.

"Another helicopter!" cried Dan. "A bigger one this time."

Excited now, the children watched.

"It's going to save the Dillons," shouted Dan. "It's coming down to their window."

But the machine did not come down. It hovered over the house, with a long rope dangling. The rope came down in front of the upstairs window. After a while, it moved away. Mrs. Dillon hung to the rope, with the loop around her arms and shoulders. The youngest child, little Frank, clung to her, his arms around her neck. The machine and the figures moved through the air.

"They are coming this way!" cried the spectators.

Sally and Barbara did not wait. They ran back to the Boyd house.

"Mother! Mother!" they cried. "Oh Mother, do come quick!"

The two women came rushing out of the house.

"The Dillons are being rescued," said the girls, pointing.

The women looked up and saw the helicopter coming over.

"Oh, that poor woman," said Mrs. Graham. "Do you suppose they'll bring all those children over like that?"

They watched the machine. It came down closer and closer. The man in it was making gestures to the people on the ground.

"He wants to land her here," said Mrs. Boyd.

"Yes, it's coming lower," said Mrs. Graham.

The two women rushed to Mrs. Dillon as her feet touched the ground. She had fainted and now fell into Mrs. Boyd's arms. Mrs. Graham took little Frank. The Civil Defense man, who had returned, took the rope off them both.

"I want my baby! I want my baby!" cried Mrs. Dillon. The child was put in her arms again.

"Won't you come in my house and lie down?" asked Mrs. Boyd.

"Oh, my children! Where are they?" cried Mrs. Dillon.

Two by two the Dillons were rescued. Clinging to the long rope, they were carried through the air and brought down to safety—to friends.

Mrs. Boyd brought Mrs. Dillon and sick Mary and the ailing babies into her house. She gave them coffee and milk. She found pillows and blankets for them and they lay down to rest.

All but the boys, Tommy and Mike. They stayed outside and talked about their ride through the air.

"I bet you were scared," said Sally.

"No, I liked it," said Tommy. "It was fun."

He did not sound like the old Tommy she had known before.

3

SCHOOL BY DAY

The children crowded round the Dillon boys in the rain. It was exciting to see a boy who had had a helicopter ride. Tommy did not act silly today. His face looked white and he was serious.

"Why didn't you folks leave your house before?" asked Dan.

"We got home real late last night," said Tommy. "Me and Mike and my Daddy went to a movie, and when we got home we went to bed."

"Couldn't you hear when the policeman banged on your door?" asked Dan.

"They came once and told us to go back to bed," said Tommy. "They said they'd watch and see how high the river came and come back and tell us. My father was up at two o'clock. The water was going down then, so he went back to bed. At three o'clock the water came back up again, but the police never came to tell us. They must have gone to sleep in their duck."

"No," said Dan. "The men have been rescuing people all night in boats, my father, too. That motorboat tipped over about four times, trying to get to your house. We watched it."

"They went off and left us," said Tommy, sniffling.

"What about that rope?" asked Sally. "We saw the men throw a long rope in your upstairs window."

"My Dad tied it around the chimney in our bedroom closet," said Tommy. "That will keep the house from washing away, he said."

"What about my compact?" asked Sally. "Was that downstairs or upstairs?"

"I dunno—I forget—" said Tommy, mumbling. "Don't know just where I put it . . ."

"Come, children, we must go," called Mrs. Boyd from the front door.

The children ran up to the Boyd house.

"Oh, Mother," cried Barbara, "*we* don't have to leave, do we?"

"Yes," said Mrs. Boyd. "I promised we'd go as soon as the Dillons were saved."

Mrs. Dillon was up now, gathering her children around her.

"Where are we going? To Uncle Paul's?" asked Sally.

"No," said Mrs. Graham. "We can't get through—the bridges

are out. The Civil Defense man told us to go to Union School. They are taking in people there."

"But *our* house is not flooded, Mother," said Barbara. "Why do *we* have to go? Can't the Dillons and the Grahams stay here with us?"

Mrs. Boyd did not stop to explain. She told the Dillons to get in her car and she drove off with them. In half an hour she was back for the Grahams. As they drove out to the highway, they could see that the water was deep under the railroad trestle. The banks on both sides had been washed away. The tracks were sagging low across the opening. No cars could come through from Hartford.

Along the highway, everything looked different. The river had cut in much closer to the road. Houses were gone and trees were floating. It was a scene of desolation. Mrs. Boyd drove through deep water all the way. She parked her car and they all got out.

Union School stood on a high hill, overlooking the river valley. Sally hardly knew where she was. The school looked like some place she had never been before. Cars and trucks were parked in front. A fire engine stood by the door. Firemen and Civil Defense workers were giving and taking messages. People were going in and out of the building. No one spoke to the Grahams or the Boyds. No one smiled. It was still pouring rain.

The two women herded the children inside. A number of families were already there. A Civil Defense worker with a white helmet on his head was telling them what to do.

"All refugees will find mats in the gymnasium," he said, "in case you want to rest. Army cots will soon be here and food is on

the way. Come in and make yourselves comfortable."

Sally pulled her mother's arm.

"Are we *refugees?*" she asked. "I thought all the refugees were in Europe or Korea."

Mother smiled a little. "We used to read about those poor people in the paper," she said. "Now we know how it feels ourselves."

It seemed strange to come to school so early in the morning. The electricity was off, so the halls and classrooms looked gloomy and deserted. Sally opened the door of her Fourth Grade room. The shades were pulled down, but some of the children's drawings still hung on the wall. What a happy place it had been

—last year, even if Tommy Dillon did pull her hair every day.

She closed the door quickly, then followed the other children to the kitchen. They were hungry, looking for something to eat. Mrs. Graham emptied her basket, and other women who had brought food, did the same. They found dishes in the cupboard and filled them with what they had.

"What's this? Cold soup?" cried Tommy Dillon, holding up his spoon in disgust.

Sally turned on him. "If you don't like it," she said, "you're not very hungry, Tommy Dillon."

"I like my soup *hot*!" said Tommy.

Dan Boyd spoke up. "Go find a stove and cook it."

The children laughed and went on eating. The milk was divided and each child got a taste. Then Helen Dillon, Tommy's oldest sister, set the children to work. Sally and Barbara washed dishes, Tommy and Dan dried them.

People kept coming in and asking questions. Some direction was needed, so Mrs. Boyd took charge, with Mrs. Graham her willing helper. Mrs. Dillon was lying down in the gymnasium. Mrs. Boyd was good at making decisions. Soon she was telling people what to do. She did not realize that before the next day was over, two hundred and fifty people would be cared for in the school.

Everything began to happen at once, as more people were brought in. Mrs. Graham unpacked cartons of groceries brought by a helicopter. Men brought in pails of water, hauled from springs up in the hills. All water had to be boiled before it could be used, and there was no way to boil it. The stove was electric and there was no current. A man came in and asked how many cots and blankets would be needed.

Sally walked through the halls with her arm around Karen, who was still hugging her big rag doll. Everybody was busy but the children. Barbara Boyd came up.

"What did we come here for?" asked Sally. "I wish we had stayed at your house."

"So do I," said Barbara. "It was more fun there."

"We can't do a thing here," said Sally.

"Let's try to think of something," said Barbara.

The door opened and a National Guard soldier came in, carrying a huge carton on his back.

"What you got there?" asked Barbara.

"Clothing from the Salvation Army," the soldier said. "Where shall I put it?"

Barbara was as good as her mother at making decisions. She thought quickly. "Right here," she said. "We've been waiting for you."

"You have?" The soldier looked at the girls and laughed. He dropped the carton at the end of the hall and went out.

"Why did he laugh at us?" asked Sally.

"I suppose we look funny," said Barbara.

The girls looked at each other. Not till then did they realize how strangely they were dressed.

Sally wore big rubbers, her oldest dress, her father's oldest hat on her head and her mother's big loose sweater around her shoulders, pinned with a safety pin. Barbara looked strange too. She still wore her everyday dress covered by her mother's apron and her old red topcoat. Karen wore a coat of Bobby's and had galoshes on her feet.

"I can't help it—" said Sally. "I've got nice clothes at home, but maybe they're washed away now."

"What do you care?" said Barbara. She pointed to the carton. "Let's open that box and see what's inside."

The carton was four feet square and about three feet high. It was filled with clothes all neatly folded.

"Let's get dressed up," Barbara went on.

Sally and Karen needed no encouragement. "And play *ladies*!" they added.

The soldier came back with a large box of shoes. He grinned at the girls again and went out. The girls lost no time in looking over the clothes. They took things out and dropped what they didn't want on the floor.

"Here's two dresses for my baby sister!" cried Sally, holding them up.

A woman came out of a classroom.

"Don't touch those clothes, children," she said and hurried away.

"We don't hear too good, do we, Barbara?" said Sally laughing.

The girls found ladies' skirts and blouses and put them on. They took off their rubbers and put on high-heeled shoes. They paraded through the hall.

They were having great fun when the boys came up. Sally's little brothers, Jack and Tim, were with the Dillon boys. Sally walked away when she saw Tommy Dillon appear.

"What you girls doin'?" asked Tommy. "Helpin' yourselves to new clothes?" He picked up a boy's shirt off the pile. "These ain't new clothes. These are old cast-offs that people didn't want any more."

He followed the girls and jeered at them. The other boys tagged along.

"Look at the pretty young ladies, all dressed up in high heels!" Tommy teased. "Don't you wish you had a pocketbook with a pretty *compact* in it, so you could powder your nose?"

"I *hate* you, Tommy Dillon!" cried Sally. "You're *mean!*"

The girls hurried into the gymnasium. Other children were there, waiting or playing listlessly. They closed the door behind them. When the boys did not come to open it, the girls went to the stage and pretended to act in a play in front of the curtain. Still the boys did not come. They went back to the hall door and peeked out.

"Look! Tommy Dillon is taking clothes for himself!" cried Karen.

Tommy was reaching into one of the boxes, so the girls hurried back. Now, Tommy was on the floor with the other boys, all smaller than himself—his own three brothers, Mike, Donny and Frank, and Sally's little brothers, Jack and Tim. Bobby was helping him. Rusty the dog was there too.

"What are you doing, Tommy Dillon?" demanded Sally. "Taking clothes and shoes for yourself without asking anybody?"

Tommy held up a small pair of shoes. He pointed to the little boys' feet. He spoke seriously now.

"All these little kids was barefooted. Their feet was wet and

cold. I found shoes and socks for 'em—just the right size. That's what these clothes and shoes are for—for the people who lost everything."

Sally could not find a word to say. Jack and Tim showed her their new shoes and socks. She nodded, admiring. Then she saw Barbara Boyd taking off her grown-up clothes. Barbara folded them neatly and put them back in the carton.

"What you taking them off for?" asked Sally.

Barbara did not answer. Tommy was looking through the clothing box again. Barbara was helping him. She asked him what size he wore. They found two shirts, a pair of dungarees, shoes and socks that looked just right. Tommy put them in a little pile.

The same lady came back to the same classroom again. She

stopped and said to Tommy, "You can't have those, boy. You didn't lose anything."

Tommy's mouth dropped open. "I didn't?"

Barbara spoke up. "Oh yes, he did," she said. "He was rescued by helicopter. He lost *everything*."

The woman said nothing more. She went in the classroom and closed the door behind her.

Sally's brother, Bobby, began digging in the box. He found a piece of fur and tied it round his head. Jack and Tim chased him, calling him *Davy*.

Bobby said, "See my fuzzy-buzzy! No, I'm not Davy—I didn't kill no b'ar!"

The door of the Principal's office opened, and a large woman came down the hall. She had black hair and fierce black eyes behind her glasses. She bore down upon the children before they had time to move.

"What's this? What are you children doing?" she cried. "Have you been fooling around with the clothing? Who told you you could open these boxes?"

None of them answered.

"Go to the gymnasium, all of you," she ordered. "The children are to stay in the gymnasium. They are not allowed in the halls."

Sheepishly, the children walked away. They went back to the gym.

"That's Mrs. Bradford," said Barbara. "She's president of the PTA."

Sally still wore her "lady" clothes. "Why didn't you keep yours?" she asked.

"I'm tired of playing that," said Barbara. "It's too babyish."

Without a word, Sally took off her skirt, blouse and high-heeled slippers. "What can I do with them?" she asked.

"Go put them back in the clothing box," said Barbara.

"But what if Mrs. Bradford sees me?" asked Sally.

"Just tell her you're sorry," said Barbara.

Sally ran down the hall and tossed the clothes in the box. The woman was gone, so no one noticed.

4

STILL AT SCHOOL

Look at those kids!" said Sally.

Back in the gymnasium, the children were playing. The boys turned somersaults on the mats. They got up in the bleachers and jumped down, turning flipflops on the mats.

Sally, Karen and Barbara and some of the other girls played hide-and-seek on the stage. It was dark back of the curtain, and they bumped around, hitting their heads on water pipes. Ruth Nelson brought a flashlight and tried shining it in their faces. The Nelsons, another River Bend family, had just been brought in.

There were two pianos on the stage. Tommy Dillon and Jerry Nelson started drumming on them. Rusty jumped and barked loudly. Then, afraid the noise would be heard and somebody would come in, the boys ran and hid under the seats. Karen and Ruth Nelson played with Karen's rag doll. While they were playing, the children forgot all about the flood.

At last Sally got tired of tearing around. When the gymnasium door opened to let more children in, she slipped out. She walked through the halls quietly, hoping no one would notice her. She was lonesome for her mother, but could not find her.

Other women were in the kitchen cooking now, and the cafeteria tables were full. Was it lunch time? Sally had no idea. The

big clock on the wall was not going. It said two o'clock. Was that afternoon or the night before? The place smelled of coffee—everybody was drinking it. Oil stoves had been brought in and it was being served hot.

Then Sally saw Tommy Dillon.

"The Red Cross sent in plenty of food," he told her. "You can have all you want—if they got it!"

"Is it hard to get?" asked Sally.

"No," said Tommy. "Just sit down and they bring you something. The food's *hot* now. They've got stoves to cook on."

Tommy and Jerry sat down and soon they were eating. They had spaghetti, peaches and apple cider. Sally sat down on the other side.

"We been here five times," Tommy whispered across the table. "Nobody keeps track of how many times we eat." He pressed his stomach. "Gee! This tastes good."

Jerry Nelson walked over to a table and got a bottle of soda and a dish of melted ice cream. He poured the soda on the ice cream and called it Sunday-pop. "The helicopter brought crates of cold drinks," he said.

"Nobody counts how many sodas you drink," said Tommy. "Us kids are having about fifteen each. I've had strawberry, sarsaparilla, raspberry . . ."

"Why do you drink all that?" asked Sally.

"It's hot today," said Tommy, "and there's no water."

Sally did not get spaghetti. A woman brought her cornflakes, but she was tired of them, so she went out. In the hall stood two large Army jugs with taps. People were crowding around to get

drinks. Tommy Dillon was wrong. There was water, after all.
A woman handed out paper cups. Sally was waiting in line, when
Tommy Dillon pushed in in front of her.

"Go ahead," she said, "if you're in such a hurry."

"Oh for a drink of cold water!" cried Tommy.

He filled his cup and took a drink. He made an ugly face and
said to the woman, "I asked for cold water and you gave me hot."

Sally said, "Isn't that just too bad!" She drank her own.

The woman explained, "We boiled it and it hasn't cooled off
yet. We have no ice and no icebox. So you'll have to drink it
warm."

"It's still wet," said the next man in line.

Sally wandered in the hall. The classrooms were open now,
filled with people, most of them strangers to her. They were all

talking about the flood and what a hard time they had and the things that had washed away. All they could do was eat all day. If they did not want to eat, they could just sit. Volunteer workers were hurrying back and forth, trying to help. In the gymnasium, mothers were putting young children down for naps. She saw her mother and baby Betty, both sleeping. A woman told everybody to keep quiet. Sally was too restless to sleep, so she went out again.

A sick boy on a stretcher was carried into the health room. Soon Dr. Otis came out, saying, "He's getting the virus." But he was called back in again. As Sally passed the door, the black-haired woman with the beady eyes, spotted her. Sally darted away, but the woman came and took her by the arm.

"Here," she said. "You know where the gym is, don't you?"

"Yes," said Sally. Her heart was in her mouth. Was she going to be scolded for walking in the hall?

"Take this girl back to the gym with you," said Mrs. Bradford.

An older girl of about thirteen, in wet and muddy clothes, came out. She was sobbing and crying bitterly. Her red and mottled face was hidden under her tangled black curls.

"I won't go!" she said. "You can't make me. I'm going back home and stay there till I find my little sister. They took my mother to the hospital and . . ."

"You can't go back, Angela," said Mrs. Bradford patiently. "Your home isn't there any more. Your little sister will be brought in any time now, just as you were. The helicopter is sure to find her."

"Linda! Linda! Oh, Linda!" called Angela. "Oh why did I

ever go away and leave her? *Linda! Linda!*"

When the girl lifted her face, Sally saw that it was Angela
Marciano. She remembered seeing Angela and little Linda in the
River Bend store—was it only yesterday? And now Linda was
lost. Sally wanted to comfort Angela but did not know how.
Shyly she took her hand to walk down the hall with her. Angela
looked up at her once, but did not seem to recognize her.

"Angela, don't you know me? I'm Sally Graham." But Angela
gave no sign that she heard.

Mrs. Bradford told the doctor about the Marcianos. Angela
and her mother and two brothers and little sister had been
taken from their home by two volunteer firemen in a boat. When
the boat overturned, the family managed to climb on the roof
of a floating house. The two firemen were with them. When the

roof collapsed, they clung to trees until rescued by a helicopter. The second fireman, Leo Rogers, with Linda in his arms, swam for a tree farther away. But no one had seen him or the child again.

"Do you want something to eat, Angela?" asked Sally, starting toward the cafeteria. "That will make you feel better."

The girl's eyes filled with tears. "No! No!" she cried. "I want Linda! My little sister, Linda! When are they going to find her? I've got to go back and see. I won't eat until they find her."

She broke away from Sally and ran back to the front of the building. Mrs. Bradford heard her cries and brought her into the health room again.

"Come, come now," said Dr. Otis, "this won't do, Angela. Lie down here and rest a while."

He gave the girl a sedative. She stopped crying, lay down on the cot and became quiet.

Sally went back to the gymnasium, feeling sorry for Angela. As she passed the boxes of clothing, she saw two women sorting them into piles. They were choosing clothes for the Marciano family.

In Sally's concern over Angela, she forgot about looking for her mother. Now suddenly, Mrs. Graham appeared in the hall. Barbara Boyd was with her and Barbara held baby Betty in her arms. Barbara took the bottle from Mrs. Graham and went back into the gym to feed the baby.

"Where have you been, Sally?" asked Mother. "I wanted you to help with the baby. I had to ask Barbara to give her her bottle."

Sally put her arms around her mother's waist and began to cry.

"When are we going home, Mother?" she sobbed.

"I don't know, Sally," said Mother. "Let me go now. There are people here who need me. I must go and help them."

"*I* need you, Mother," cried Sally. "Don't go away and leave me."

Mrs. Graham sat down and talked to Sally.

"You are warm and well-fed and dry here," she said. "Many people are in real distress. They are sick, hurt, half-drowned, homeless. Have you thought of them?"

Sally hung her head and did not answer.

"Don't act like a baby," said Mother. "I depend on you to be an example to your brothers and sister."

"Linda Marciano must be drowned, Mother," said Sally. "Angela says they can't find her anywhere. Don't you care? What if it was Karen?"

"Stop worrying," said Mother. "Worry won't bring Linda back. Go and stay with the other children. Look after Jack and Tim. Help Barbara with the baby."

As Sally returned to the gymnasium, she saw a man with his arm in a sling. He sat huddled over, unhappy. He was worse off than she. Her arm was not broken. He looked so sad, she asked him, "How do you feel today?"

The man looked up, surprised, and said, "I'll be better pretty soon."

"How did you get hurt?" Sally asked.

"I hit some wires when I was swinging on that long rope," the man said. "It broke my arm and a couple of ribs." He smiled and added, "But I'm still alive."

"I'm sorry you broke your arm," said Sally. Her concern for herself had now widened to include concern for others.

Back in the gymnasium, she sat down beside Barbara and played with baby Betty for a while. Then she went over to the window where the boys were looking out.

"Gee! Look out there!" cried Barbara's brother Ronnie. "That old chopper's working overtime. It keeps on bringin' people in."

"What do you know—it's stopped raining!" cried Tommy Dillon. "Let's go outside. We're missing everything by staying in here."

The boys went exploring, looking for an unlocked window. Soon they found one, in the small room offstage. Sally followed and watched them jump out one by one. The window was on the rear of the building, so no one saw them. The boys crept round the corner to watch the excitement.

Sally came back and whispered to Barbara. The baby had fallen asleep now beside Mrs. Dillon, who was resting. Karen was sleeping, too, with her rag doll in her arms and Rusty curled up at her feet. Sally and Barbara went into the stage room and climbed to the window sill. Like the boys, they jumped down. They crept up to the edge of the crowd. The people were listening to reports coming in on the radio on the fire engine:

"John Ferguson wants Alonzo Patterson to know that his hogs are O. K., safe in the barn . . . Mrs. Ralph Woods on Liberty Street will house a homeless family. The J. T. Websters are O. K. and can take in neighbors . . . Get in touch with the Red Cross about food, shelter and clothing . . . The Governor of Connecticut is flying over towns in the Naugatuck and Farmington River valleys to learn the extent of the damage. Hundreds of homes have been washed away, stores and industries wiped out . . ."

"It's a real flood all right," said the man next to Sally.

"Go to the Town Hall . . . ask your Civil Defense worker what you should do," the radio voice went on. "Boil all water for ten minutes, no matter what the source, whether from spring, shallow well or artesian well. Boil all water ten minutes before using. Use one-half pound chloride of lime in three gallons of water for disinfecting . . . We urge you to stay off the roads. Stay in your home if you still have one . . . The three children of R. T. Webb of River Bend are reported missing . . ."

Sally knew the little Webb boys. They had often played with Jack and Tim. "The Webb boys too!" said Barbara.

"They didn't say anything about Linda," said Sally.

The girls went over where the boys were. Ray and Ralph Marberry were there and Tony Marciano was talking to Ronnie and Tommy.

"Me and Al floated on our backs," said Tony, "like the firemen do, till we came to the railroad trestle. Angela was still hangin' in the tree. I told her not to let go. When we got up on the tracks, I waved and the man saw us and come and got us. He got both of us and my mother and Angela out of the trees . . ."

"How'd you like it hangin' on a long rope?" asked Tommy Dillon.

"Ugh!" said Tony. "I sure was scared. They can't find my little sister anywhere. They left her in a tree . . ."

A helicopter came over the school, then lowered to make a

landing. A man and a woman got out. It was the Webbs without their children. Tears ran down the woman's face.

"I don't like this," said Sally. "Let's go back. Floods are no fun at all."

"We can't ever get back up to that window," said Barbara. "It's too high off the ground."

"What will we do?" asked Sally.

Just then Sally saw her father talking to one of the firemen. Both men saw the girls at once.

"Go back in the gymnasium and stay there," called Mr. Graham. "Don't let me see you out here again!" He called the boys and sent them in too.

The children went in the front door and hurried to the gymnasium. They hated the place now more than ever. It was filled with crying babies.

5

SCHOOL BY NIGHT

Where's Daddy, Mother?" asked Sally.

"He and Mr. Dillon went to Farmington to get flashlights and candles. I don't know when he'll get back."

"Do we have to go to bed *here*," asked Karen, "with all these people?"

"Yes," said Mother. "We'll take our shoes and stockings off and leave our clothes on. Then we'll lie down on these cots."

Sally and Karen helped the little boys get ready for bed. They both shared a cot, Jack at the head and Tim at the foot. They kicked each other, then started tickling until Mother shushed them. Bobby curled up on a cot with Rusty in his arms.

Mrs. Graham and the girls put two cots together. Sally's baby sister slept between her and her mother, so she would not roll over and hurt her head. Karen slept on the other side of Sally. The baby cried once, but Mother gave her a bottle and she was all right.

The gymnasium looked stranger now than ever. Five long rows of Army cots, standing side by side, filled the floor. Here and there were baby cribs on wheels. Army blankets had been given out. Women and children in all stages of dress and undress were trying to make themselves comfortable. Some sat on the cots, doing nothing. Some laughed and talked. Others walked briskly around. A few sobbed and cried, thinking of the homes they no longer had and wondering what was to become of them. The room grew quieter as more and more families settled down for the night.

There were no men. All of them were out helping with rescue work. Outside it was raining again. The rain made a steady tattoo on the roof.

As darkness fell, a woman came in with flashlights, candles and matches. Sally wondered if her father had brought them, but she did not like to ask. Soon, soft lights were glowing here and there over the room. Sleeping with strangers was a new experience for all. Sally lay awake long after Karen and the little ones had fallen asleep.

Sleeping beside the Grahams was an old lady with a child. Sally did not know them. The Nelsons were in the next row and

LOIS LENSKI

the Boyds and Dillons across the room. Sally sat up in bed several times and waved to Barbara. After the room got dark, it looked spooky with flashlights going off and on. Sally could see Ruth Nelson holding a flashlight up to a comic book, trying to read it.

Sally began talking to Mother in a low voice.

"Is our house gone?" she asked.

"I don't know if we have a house or not," said Mother. "Daddy will tell us as soon as he finds out."

"When are we going back home?" asked Sally.

"I don't know that either," said Mother. "We have food, drink and shelter here. We must thank God for that."

Sally lay quiet for a time. Then she turned to Mother and said, "Oh, I want to go home . . . I don't like it here."

Mother reached over and patted her. "Go to sleep, dear," she said. "You'll feel better in the morning."

Sally kept turning over and back again.

"You're not scared, are you?" asked Mother.

"Not with you by me," said Sally.

"Say your prayers, dear, and go to sleep," said Mother.

The last thing Sally heard before going to sleep was Mother telling the boys to lie still. The next thing she knew some one was shaking her. She opened her eyes—and it was Barbara. Morning had come. Sally was surprised to find herself still at school.

The next day was busier than ever. All morning, the people stood in line in the hall by the health room. Dr. Otis and several nurses in white caps were there giving shots. Everybody had to take one to avoid getting typhoid fever. The Grahams all stood in line and waited. Mother carried baby Betty, and Sally and

Karen held Jack and Tim by the hand. Bobby brought up the rear, with Rusty in his arms. At last they got inside, and their turns came. The doctor was quick and the pricks did not hurt much. Only Tim cried.

When they came out in the hall, there was Daddy. Mother and the children gathered round to hear his news.

"Have we got a house or not?" asked Bobby.

"We still have a house," said Daddy.

"Thank God," said Mother.

Mr. Graham had had to travel a roundabout way to the Town Hall in the center of town, to get his pass. He found a friend to take him in a canoe down Farmington Avenue, to see if the house was still there. The waters had receded somewhat. From the boat he could look into the broken windows.

"You didn't bring us any clothes?" asked Mother.

"I couldn't get the doors or windows open," said Daddy. "They are all swollen shut. I might have got in the upstairs window if I'd had a ladder."

"How was the house?" asked Mother.

"There's still water downstairs," said Daddy. "The piano is lying face down—it must have bounced around. Your cedar chest floated out to the kitchen. The table is still upright, with the new coffeemaker on it. It must have gone up and down again. The washing machine moved around and ended up in a corner. Most of the windows are broken. It's a good thing the cellar door was left open. That's why we still have a house. The pressure was the same inside as out."

"How deep was the water?" asked Mother.

"It must have been over six feet," said Daddy. "We're lucky it didn't reach the second floor."

"And the rest of town?" asked Mother.

"There are only four houses left on the river side of Farmington Avenue," said Daddy. "It's the saddest sight you want to see. Trash and lumber, ruined cars and trucks, debris everywhere."

"Only four houses!" cried Mother. "All the others?"

"Washed away," said Daddy. "Most of those on New Britain Avenue too."

"Oh Daddy," cried Sally. "Can't we go home now? The water must be all down by today, if it was starting to go down last night."

"We can't go till we are allowed to," said Daddy. "I had to get a pass to even go and look at it."

"But Daddy," said Karen. "We can't stay *here*. There's too many people. Where are we going then?"

"I'll tell you later," said Daddy.

"Let's go to Maine," said Jack.

"I wish we could," said Daddy.

Sally was out in front of the school when a car drove up and everybody crowded around it. She went over to see. There was Fireman Leo Rogers and little Linda Marciano with her dog Tiny. The people went wild.

"Linda Marciano! Linda has been rescued!" they cried.

Sad-faced, weeping Angela was told the news. She rushed out of the school, gathered her small sister in her arms and wept now for joy. The little dog, Tiny, barked and barked. The fireman told his story, and everybody listened.

He and Linda and the dog had been swept some distance from the rest of the family. Rogers put Linda into a tree, then took the belt off her dress and tied her to a branch. She held the dog in her arms. From boards floating by, the fireman made a makeshift raft. It was so shaky, he was afraid to trust it with the child. Leaving her in the tree, he called, "Wait for me, Linda. I'll be back." But it was a long time before he saw her again. He rode his raft until it collapsed beneath him.

"I decided to swim for it," he said. "Then by the grace of God an inner tube floated by. That helped a lot."

After swimming several miles, he finally made it to dry land. He hurried to the Farmington Firehouse and made arrangements to go up in a helicopter. Trip after trip was made, but there was no trace of Linda. The search continued all day Friday, but still Linda could not be found.

Rescue workers refused to give up the search. Late into the night, boats continued to go out, looking for the child. At five in the morning, Saturday, Rogers set out once more in his canoe. Six hours later, at eleven o'clock, he found Linda. She was playing in the sand under the tree with her dog Tiny. She had untied her belt and climbed down after the waters receded. She had waited nearly thirty hours for him to come. Smiling up at the fireman, she said, "I thought you were never coming back, but you did!"

He took her to shore in his canoe. Now she was reunited with her older sister and her brothers Tony and Al.

Linda was the center of attention. All the people crowded round to ask her questions. A newspaper reporter asked her if she would appear on television.

Linda looked down at her torn and muddy dress, at her bare black feet. "How can I?" she said.

Then Dr. Otis came and took her in the building. She was taken to the health room for examination and rest. Later she was carried to the same hospital where her mother was.

After the excitement over Linda died down, Sally had a head-ache. Mother told her to lie down on a cot in the gymnasium. Barbara and Karen begged her to come and play with them, but she did not feel like it. She could not eat, either.

"I feel sick," she said.

"It must be the shot," said Mother.

Other children were lying on cots and mats. They did not play as hard as on the previous day. The shots were beginning to have their effect. Some were sick at their stomachs.

When Sally woke up from a restless sleep, she heard Daddy and Mother talking about going somewhere. If only she could go home again.

"Are we going home?" she asked.

"No, dear," said Mother. "You heard what Daddy said."

"I want to go home," said Sally.

"So do we all," said Mother.

The day passed somehow, and another night came. Sally was walking around now, though her arm still pained her.

"Let's go outside," she said to Barbara.

The Army men had lamps and chairs outside. The weather was still hot, and the night was close. Stars were shining, but people said the rain was not over. The girls sat down under the stars to get some fresh air. It was nice to see the stars shining. Maybe the sun would come out tomorrow. It would be good to see the sun again, after all the long days of rain.

A soldier came up and said, "We need those chairs."

So the girls got up and went in.

"Where are we going?" asked Sally.

The question was in the minds of all the children.

"I'm going home," said Barbara Boyd. "We only had water in the cellar, and the fire department is there now pumping it out."

Sally and Karen looked so sad, Barbara felt sorry for them.

"Ask your mother if you can come home with me," said Barbara.

Sally shook her head. "Mother won't let us. She says, whatever happens, we're all going to stay together."

By Saturday night, the river had gone down. The stream, which had been a raging torrent for two days and two nights, seemed to have emptied itself, and was now a tiny harmless trickle of water in a riverbed of rocks, boulders and debris.

For sanitary reasons, all the families had to be evacuated from Union School. Many homeless people had already left, to go to friends on higher ground. Those who had no cars were to be given transportation.

Again the halls and gymnasium were scenes of disorder. Army cots, temporary oil stoves and folding chairs were being moved out. Food and medical supplies were being taken to Red Cross headquarters in the Town Hall. All was noise and confusion.

Sally heard a group of mothers talking.

"I'm not going," said Mrs. Dillon. Her seven children were huddled around her. "They're just taking us to another school. I can't go on living like this. My husband is trying to find some one to take us to Vermont, to his parents. We have no car and no way to get there."

Mrs. Bradford, the black-eyed woman, came up.

"The larger families will be broken up," she said, "and taken to private homes. We have had offers from many people in the high part of town. They are willing and anxious to take you into their homes, but not many of them can accommodate a family of seven or more people. Your children will be well cared for . . ."

"But mine are sick . . ." said one woman.

"We have only the clothes we are wearing," said another woman.

"Food and clothing will be available at the Town Hall," said Mrs. Bradford. "Don't worry about that."

"Can they take me and my family to Winsted?" asked Mrs. Nelson. "My sister lives there. She'll take us in."

"It is impossible to get to Winsted," said Mrs. Bradford. "Winsted is hard hit. All the roads to the north are blocked. The only way to get even to Farmington is by Army duck."

"I'm going to keep my kids with me," said Mrs. Dillon. "We're going to Vermont. My husband will find a way to get there."

Slowly the women turned away. They herded their children and their few possessions out the door, where an Army duck stood waiting. The "duck" was a heavy cumbersome vehicle, constructed by the U. S. Army for land or water transportation.

"Is that a *duck*?" asked Sally. "I thought it was something that could fly."

"No, it swims, silly," said her brother Bobby. "It can float and also go on wheels. It's a boat and a car for river or road."

Women and children were being helped up the sides of the strange vehicle. It was surprising how many people the duck could hold. More and more got in.

"All families going to Wallace School come this way," said the Civil Defense director.

Soon the duck moved off down the hill and onto the highway. Another took its place. When it was loaded, a third one came.

Several cars drove up. "All families going to friends in the high part of town will be taken in these cars. Come this way," said the director.

The cars were quickly filled.

Mrs. Dillon refused to go in the duck and refused to go in the cars. Then Mr. Dillon came up.

"My wife don't want our kids scattered," he told the director, "and she don't want to go to another school. I have a friend who works at the Benton Sand and Gravel Co. on Red Brick Road. That's between Unionville and Farmington. He'll give me a car, I think, to drive to my folks in Vermont."

"Come on," said the director. "We'll drop you off at Red Brick Road."

The Dillons big and little, climbed into the last duck. Tommy turned around with a flourish and waved a gay good-bye.

"Last call for transportation to Farmington!" called the director.

Mrs. Graham hurried up, holding sick Sally by the hand and the baby in her arms. Bobby and Karen pulled Jack and Tim along. Rusty, as usual, was in Bobby's arms, and Karen's doll in hers. They started toward the duck. Mrs. Graham had decided to go along with the other families, since she could not return to their own home.

Sally had not seen Barbara and wondered where she was. She hated to go to Farmington without telling Barbara good-bye.

Suddenly Mrs. Boyd came rushing up.

"Oh, Carrie," she cried. "You're not going there. You are coming to our house. My husband came back with our car, and I drove over. The house is all right and we have permission to stay there. I've taken the Nelsons over and now I've come for you."

"But will you have room for six children," asked Mrs. Graham, "if you have the Nelsons too?"

"We'll *make* room," said Mrs. Boyd. "We'll double up and the boys can sleep on the floor. I can't let you go off to another school with that sick girl and those little ones. You're coming to us."

For the first time since Thursday night, Mrs. Graham began to cry.

"Oh, Alice," she said, "what a good friend you are. The doctor has given Sally aureomycin, and she must be put to bed where I can watch her. It might be typhoid . . . or polio. She must be watched carefully."

A soldier lifted sick Sally into Mrs. Boyd's car. The boys were quiet and well behaved. The baby did not cry and the dog did not bark. All were happy to be going to the Boyds. It was wonderful to have good friends.

As soon as the car reached the Boyd home on the hill, Sally was taken indoors. Mrs. Nelson and Ruth were waiting to welcome the newcomers. The other children stood on the porch and looked around. Everything was changed. The neighbors' houses on the streets toward the river were gone. There was a great waste of sand where the Dillon house had stood.

Mrs. Boyd talked to the children. "You must all stay on the sun porch," she said. "No one without a pass is allowed to wander around."

The children promised to obey. They were not allowed in the back yard either. From the window they could see that it was filled with overturned trees and bushes, stacks of lumber, wrecked cars and machinery and other things that had been washed down the river.

"There's enough lumber out there to build a house," said Dan.

"Gee!" said Ronnie. "I wonder where my bike is. I hope I didn't leave it out in the yard. I hope it's not buried under all that junk."

But, inside the house, nothing was disturbed. It was clean, peaceful and comfortable. A home had never looked so good before. The children and grownups could, for a time at least, forget the destruction outside. The three women set to work at once, getting cots, couches and beds ready for the night.

Barbara tiptoed upstairs to see Sally asleep in a comfortable bed. Sally opened her eyes and asked, "What's the noise?"

"The firemen's pump," said Barbara. "They're pumping out the cellar."

Barbara brought her some food on a tray, but Sally shook her head.

"I'm not hungry," she said, "but I'm glad to be here."

Barbara held Sally's hand. "I'm glad you came."

6

HAVEN OF REFUGE

Can't we ever go outside?" begged Barbara's brother Ronnie.

"I'd like to go to a movie," said Dan. He stopped for a moment, then added, "—if there was one."

"No movies any more," mourned Jerry Nelson. "Oh, I hate this old flood. I wish it had never come."

"Well," said Barbara, "at least we have a house."

"Mother, can't I go along in the car with you?" begged Ronnie. "Just for the ride? I'm tired of staying in the house."

Mrs. Boyd said, "No, Ronnie, you cannot go anywhere. All of

you must stay in. You know the reason why." She went out the door and got in the car.

Sally was up and dressed now. Nothing serious had developed. She felt well, but she tired easily, so she lay on the couch in the living room, watching the other children. She thought of the times when they could jump in the family car and go wherever they pleased. She thought of the times when they lived more outdoors than in, when they explored every street and yard in River Bend. How they loved to ride their bikes down to the river for a swim or a boat ride, play cowboy and Indians together, then ride back to the store on the highway to buy ice cream. What good times they had! Now all that seemed long ago.

It was a new experience to be cooped up and to have to manufacture games out on the sun porch. There were ten children in all, not counting baby Betty—five Grahams, three Boyds and two Nelsons. Rusty, the dog, was always with them.

After Mrs. Boyd went away, the boys began to play noisily on the porch. Barbara and Karen brought a fashion magazine and settled on the floor by Sally's couch. Karen kept her big cloth doll close beside her. The girls had scissors and they started cutting out pretty ladies. But the boys made so much noise, the girls could not talk.

Barbara went to the door of the porch.

"Boys, don't be so noisy!" she said. "We can't hear a thing."

The boys went on playing and shouting. Rusty barked furiously. Barbara went back to them.

"What are you playing?" she demanded.

"We're playing Crash-Up-on-a-Bike!" shouted Bobby.

"I'm playing Reckless Driver!" said Jerry Nelson.

"And I'm a Space-Ship Acrobat!" cried Ronnie.

Barbara laughed and told the girls, "They're smashing up the whole world, I think."

So it wasn't as quiet and peaceful at the Boyd's house as Sally had expected. But she was happy to be there instead of at a strange school.

"Gee! I'm thirsty! I want a drink," said Ronnie.

"There's no water and you know it, Ronnie Boyd," scolded Barbara.

"I'm a camel, I live on a desert," said Bobby Graham, "and if I don't get a drink of water, I'll die."

"There's some water in the birdbath," said Barbara, looking out the window. "You might try that."

When Mrs. Boyd returned, she brought two milk cans of water. It had come from a spring in the high part of town. It had to be boiled before it could be used, and there was no stove to heat it. So there were no drinks for the children.

Mrs. Graham and the boys found scraps of wood and old newspapers. They made a small bonfire in the yard, boiling a little water in a pail. Then it had to be set aside to cool. More milk cans of water were brought for use in the bathroom.

"Use as little water as you can," said the women.

"We don't have to wash our faces, do we?" cried the boys.

"No," said Mrs. Graham.

The boys whooped with delight. Even Jack and Tim were happy about it. "No more baths, either," they cried.

"You can all stay as dirty as you like," said Barbara.

"Wash your hands in the birdbath before you eat," said Mrs. Nelson.

Sally on her couch laughed and laughed.

"Oh Mother!" said Barbara. "Look at all this mud on the rugs. All these people are tracking mud into the house, the dog too."

"Mud doesn't matter just now," said Mrs. Boyd. "We have more important things to think of. We have no food, no stove, no electricity, no water . . . and all these people in the house."

Barbara brought a broom and mop to clean up the mud.

"They might at least wipe their shoes on that old rug I put out by the door," she said.

Sally was almost asleep when Grandpa Dorsett and his wife came. Mrs. Boyd talked to them and when she found out they were homeless, she took them in. Sally moved to an easy chair, while Mrs. Boyd opened up the couch. The Dorsetts lay down and rested.

"Where is everybody going to sleep?" asked Karen, later.

The women had it all worked out. Mr. and Mrs. Graham, Sally, Karen and the baby were to take one bedroom, with double bed and cots, Mr. and Mrs. Boyd and Barbara the other bedroom. All six boys were to sleep on the floor in the sun porch. Mrs. Nelson and Ruth took the boys' small bedroom, and the Dorsetts the living-room couch.

"I never thought I could house so many," laughed Mrs. Boyd. "It's a regular house party!"

Sally counted them up. "Eighteen in all!" she said.

"Some homes up on the hills have taken in as many as forty," said Mr. Boyd. "That's what I call a full house."

"Gee! I'm hungry," said Ronnie. "When do we eat?"

"There's no electricity for cooking," said Barbara. "You know that."

"But we can't starve to death," said Bobby Graham.

"We're trying to locate a kerosene stove," said Mr. Boyd as he went out.

That first day there was nothing to eat but the same fare as before—cold soup, dry cereal without milk, canned peaches and stale cup cakes. The grownups ate in the dining alcove, and the children on the porch. They made a picnic out of it.

There was more of the same food for supper, but no one complained. When it grew dark, there were no lights. Everybody sat around for a while, then decided to go to bed.

On Monday, Mr. Graham brought word that food could be had at the Town Hall.

"I'll go do the marketing," said Dan Boyd eagerly.

"We'll go along and help," said Ronnie and Bobby.

"No," said Mr. Graham. "From here to the Town Hall is *disaster area*. No children are allowed on the streets."

"I'll go," spoke up Grandpa Dorsett. "I want to be useful. This is one thing I can do."

"But there is no car for you to use," said Mr. Graham.

"I can walk," said Grandpa. "I had two legs long before I had a car. My car is gone, but I still have my two legs. I'm slow, but I'll get there and back again."

So Grandpa Dorsett became the provider. He walked to the Town Hall to get the food. He had to go two or three times a day to get enough. But he was happy doing it. There was little change in the diet, except the addition of baked goods donated by a bakery. But it was enough. No one at the Boyd house went hungry.

Each time the men came back, they brought news. The three Webb children were still missing. Policeman Atkins and young Joe Martin had been drowned when their boat capsized. Others, too, were gone. River Bend's forty-five homes were now reduced to four. Unionville adjoining had similar serious losses. All the river towns along the Connecticut rivers, especially the Farmington and the Naugatuck, had been flooded. Not only was Connecticut affected, but parts of New Jersey, Pennsylvania and New York State. The heavy rains had come after two hurricanes, a week apart, and had left nothing but disaster in their path.

Every night at six o'clock, the town siren sounded a curfew. No one was allowed on the streets after that hour. Not only was the town a disaster area, but a health hazard as well. Grave fears were held of a possible typhoid epidemic. Darkness descended early and there was nothing to do at the Boyd house in the evenings but sit in the dark and talk.

"No lights to read by," said Barbara.

"No radio, no TV to turn on," said Ronnie.

"No movies to go to," said Dan.

"If I only had a few candles," said Mrs. Boyd, "it would be a little more cheerful. But all the stores are closed, so we cannot buy them."

"Sitting in the dark is the hardest thing of all," said Mrs. Nelson.

Mrs. Graham had gone to the Town Hall on several errands. When she returned, she had a bag full of candle stubs.

"I met Edith Johnson on the street," she said, "and she gave them to me, bless her heart!"

That night, the house party had candlelight to brighten their spirits. It was a new experience for the children. They had not used candlelight before.

"But the corners of the room stay so dark," said Barbara.

"The shadows are so big, it's spooky!" said Karen.

"Your great-grandparents had no lights but candles," Mrs. Boyd reminded them.

"And they read books in fine print," said Mrs. Graham.

"Their eyes must have been better than ours then," said Dan, picking up a magazine. "I'd have a hard time reading this."

"I'm glad I didn't live a hundred years ago," said Bobby Graham. "I prefer electricity."

"You wouldn't have known a thing about it," said Barbara. "Electricity wasn't invented yet. What if Benjamin Franklin hadn't sent up his kite?"

"Somebody else would have," said Dan. "It was bound to come."

"I think it must have been fun to dip candles in the olden days," said Sally.

"It's easier to push a button to turn on a light," said Bobby.

"To cook on a fireplace, with all the pots hanging, must have been fun too," said Barbara. "Maybe not *fun,* but interesting."

"It's easier to move the thermostat and start the oil burner going than to build a fire," said Ronnie Boyd.

"Why should everything be so *easy?*" asked Barbara.

"You're just lazy, Ronnie," said Sally. "I bet it was fun."

The lively discussion about old and new ways went on.

"Electricity is all right," said Mrs. Boyd, "but when it goes off, what then? If you had no matches, what then?"

"I'd start a fire by rubbing two sticks together," said Dan.

"And when the oil burner stops in the dead of winter," said Mrs. Graham, "how would you keep warm?"

"I'd chop down trees for fuel," said Dan. "I'd get along all right."

"Oh gee!" cried Bobby. "That's too much like work—chopping down trees."

"It's fun," said Dan. "I love to do it."

"We are all getting too soft," said Mrs. Boyd. "If our boys hate to chop wood and carry water, how can we meet disaster? How can we survive in an emergency when all these modern conveniences are cut off?"

Sitting by candlelight, they could all see each other's faces. That made it more pleasant than sitting in the dark. The boys tried a game of checkers, and the girls got out parcheesi.

When Mrs. Boyd came home one day with a kerosene lamp, the children were more excited than ever.

"To think these poor children are so ignorant, they've never seen an oil lamp before!" cried Mrs. Boyd.

"We learned about them in school when we were studying the olden days," said Sally.

"We've *seen* them in antique shops," said Barbara, "but we never knew how they worked.

Mrs. Boyd showed them how to raise and lower the wick. They took turns lighting the lamp, putting on the chimney, blowing out the flame, and lighting it again.

"When I was a girl," said Mrs. Nelson, "we lived in the country and it was my job to fill the lamps and keep the chimneys clean. I didn't enjoy it much."

"These girls are lucky!" The women laughed.

"Just press a button, that's all," said Sally.

In spite of the comforts at the Boyd house and their continued kindness, Sally could see that her mother was getting restless. She herself was becoming more homesick every day.

"Oh Mother, can't we ever go home again?" she asked.

"Yes, dear," said Mrs. Graham, "but not till the house has been cleaned up, disinfected and inspected. It's knee-deep in mud now."

"Knee-deep?" cried Sally.

"Yes, I mean it," said Mrs. Graham.

Barbara was listening. "And here I complained because people were tracking in mud on our carpet."

Each day, Mrs. Graham went away with Mrs. Boyd in her car. Mrs. Nelson stayed at the house in charge of the children.

"Everybody's getting sick in town now," Mrs. Boyd reported at the end of the week. "The typhoid shots are having their effect. Then, too, it's the cold food and funny water. People can't scrub —there's no water to scrub with. The smell down town is horrible. I had to hold my hand over my nose—sewer gas, decayed matter, disinfectants and I don't know what."

"I spent the whole morning standing in line trying to get a pass to go to *my own home*," said Mrs. Graham, discouraged. "We all need a change of clothes, since there's no water to wash anything. I haven't a cent of money and the banks are closed. I can't buy anything—the stores are closed. A person can't do a thing he wants to. He's got to take orders for everything. We might as well be in Europe."

"I met Mrs. Joruska on the street," said Mrs. Boyd. "When I said the same thing, she said they lived like this *for eleven years* in the old country."

"And here we are complaining," said Mrs. Graham, "when with us it will be only a few weeks. I'm ashamed of myself."

"It's always like this after a flood, isn't it, Mother?" asked

Sally. "Remember those floods in the Ohio River? And last year there was a bad one out in Iowa. I saw it on television."

"We have not suffered at all," said Mrs. Graham briskly. "Only those who lost dear ones and their homes, like the Webbs and the Dillons, know."

"Jim says that as soon as the town gets electricity, the stores will open from six to eight in the evening," said Mrs. Boyd. "This will allow the big trucks and bulldozers to work by day without people and traffic on the streets. After that, things will be better."

It was a happy day for all in the Boyd house, when Mr. Graham returned with a three-burner kerosene stove and several jugs of oil. He also brought a crate of eggs. The women made coffee all day long. Mrs. Nelson fried eggs on demand. Several Army men, working on bulldozers removing the debris of River Bend, stopped in now and then for food and drink.

Once after they left, Ronnie said, "That skinny guy ate twelve eggs! I counted them!"

"He must have been hungry," said Barbara.

They all laughed.

After new food supplies were brought to the Town Hall, Mrs. Graham spent one whole morning standing in line to get a piece of meat. And when she got it, it was a very tough piece of second-rate beef.

"Tough old cow that died in the flood!" said the boys.

But the women made a stew out of it, added canned vegetables, and everybody said it was the best meal they had ever eaten.

It was *meat* and it was *hot!*

7

NEW CLOTHES

We must get some new clothes," said Mrs. Graham.

"But how can we with the stores all closed?" asked Sally.

"We'll go to the Town Hall and see what they have," said her mother. "If the clothes we are wearing get any dirtier, they will fall to pieces."

"There is plenty of water now," said Mrs. Boyd.

The fire department had run a water pipe down the highway to River Bend, on top of the ground. The city water was on again. People could attach their garden hose to the pipe and get water for cleaning, washing or scrubbing. But still there was no electricity. Clothes had to be washed by hand.

"Gee! I'm sure glad to go somewhere once again," said Bobby Graham.

After being cooped up for so long, it was exciting to get out. Going somewhere meant more than it ever had before. Mrs. Boyd brought her car, and Mrs. Graham and the children got in. Barbara went along too.

"I'll tell you what I need, Mother," said Bobby. "Shoes and sweater and pants and underwear!"

"Is that all?" Mrs. Graham laughed.

"It'll do for a while," said Bobby.

Mrs. Graham turned to Karen. "Do you have to take that doll wherever you go?"

Karen hugged the doll and smiled. "Yes, I have to," she said. "Dolly wants to go too."

It was a changed town through which they passed. Most of the houses on the river side of Farmington Avenue were gone. Their back yards were gone, too, only cellar holes were left. The bridge still stood across the river, but a great gully had been washed at its far end. Across the river, houses were gone too. In those that remained, clean-up work was going on. People were shoveling out mud. Trash and debris and mud were piled high along the sidewalks. Trees on what had once been a beautiful shaded street were upturned. Stores were boarded up where plate glass windows had been.

The children were silent as they looked. Not until now did the full significance of the tragedy reach them.

Sally put her arm in her mother's. "I can't bear it," she said.

"I never thought a flood could be like this," said Barbara.

The Town Hall was a busy place. Above the door hung a huge sign: RED CROSS HEADQUARTERS. Cars were coming and going. People went in and out the door. The two women herded the children inside.

"Is this a store, Mother?" asked little Tim.

"No, it's the Town Hall, silly," said Jack.

They entered the large auditorium. On the right side were tables piled high with food, boxes of cereal and canned goods, and milk in cardboard containers. On the floor near by was an array of brooms, mops, pails, sponges and disinfectants. Mrs. Graham picked some out to take home with her. "I'll need them for cleaning up," she said.

On the left side were lines of clothes racks, with clothes hanging on hangers. There were boxes with folded clothing and shoes near by. A table in the center of the room was piled high with sheets, pillow cases and blankets. On the stage, a group of women were sitting around a table, sewing and mending second-hand clothing. Clothing had been donated and shipped in from many parts of the United States.

Mrs. Boyd helped Mrs. Graham and a volunteer worker look for clothing and shoes for the younger children. Barbara helped Karen and Sally pick out slips and dresses, second-hand shoes and socks and some underwear.

"Now, let's pick out yours," said Sally.

"Oh, I'm not taking anything," said Barbara.

"But they're *free*, Barbara," said Sally. "Look at this pretty

blouse and skirt. It's your size and your favorite color, blue."

"Why don't you take it, Barbara?" asked Karen. "You could pretend that all your clothes were lost in the flood."

"I don't need it," said Barbara. "I have enough dresses."

Sally looked at her friend in wonder. The volunteer worker said, "There are not many little girls like you. You'd be surprised how greedy people are. Most of them take all they can get, because it costs nothing."

Sally put her arm around Barbara's waist. She wished she could be as fine and good as Barbara, as thoughtful and kind.

Karen looked up at the young woman. "Can I get a dress for my doll?" she asked.

"Why yes," said the woman. She brought baby clothes and Karen chose a pink dress. She put it on her doll and thanked the woman.

"Look!" cried Barbara. "There's the Marciano girls. Let's go talk to them."

Angela Marciano came in the front door, holding her little sister Linda by the hand.

"Hi, there, Angela!" called Barbara. She and Karen and Sally went over.

"Hi!" said Angela. "What you girls doin' here? Gettin' new clothes to wear?"

"Yes," said Sally, "a few. Mine are still at home and we can't get to them."

"You getting something, Angela?" asked Barbara.

"Oh, we been here lotta times," said Angela, "and got a whole bunch of things. We got clothes for all of us and stuff to eat.

We got a dollhouse for me and Linda—Linda lets me play with it sometimes. We got games for Tony and Al. And what do you think? We got our pictures taken three times! *They're gonna be in a magazine!*"

Sally could only think of that sad day in school when Linda was missing. Now, a changed Angela was talking. And little rescued Linda was being terribly spoiled.

"Tell them what you did, Linda," bragged Angela.

"I was on TV in Hartford," said Linda, proudly. "I told 'em I stayed all night in a tree with my dog Tiny."

"Everybody thinks my little sister is wonderful," Angela went on. "We've got a rent and the Red Cross is giving us all new

furniture, beds, blankets, silverware and tables and a beautiful red chair to go good with our new green rug! Gee! There's my mother. We gotta go."

Barbara and Karen laughed happily over the good fortune of the Marcianos. They saw some of their school friends around the water cooler at the entrance. Several boys were getting drinks, while the girls waited their turn.

"There's that mean old Tommy Dillon," said Sally. "I thought the Dillons went to Vermont."

"There's David Joruska and Carol Rosansky," said Barbara. "Let's go over and talk to them."

"Hi, there!" said Tommy Dillon, as the girls came up. "Want a drink of water? It's *cold* this time."

He held out a cup of water and Sally took it. After she drank, she made a face. "It tastes funny," she said.

"Just like gasoline!" laughed Tommy. "They put Army tablets in it."

"Chlorine, probably," said Barbara.

People came up with jugs to fill, so the children moved to one side. It was their first meeting since they had left Union School after the flood. Like the adults, all the children wanted to talk. So much had happened and talk was their first outlet. Carol Rosansky was telling about her escape.

"I wasn't too scared," she said. "I never thought our house would go. My mother and father stood on a hill and watched all the houses go by. But they didn't see ours go."

"Our house went," said David Joruska. "The water took it away at nine o'clock on Flood Friday. It went floating down the street. The nails fell out of the boards and it all came apart. All the houses broke in pieces."

"How do you know?" asked Barbara. "Did you see it?"

"No," said David. "I never saw our house after it went, but my father did." He paused for a moment. "My mother said she'd never like to live near that river again."

The children were silent. Then Tommy Dillon spoke up.

"Huh!" he said. "That's nothing. Everybody's house went. Ours went too." He spoke proudly, in a bragging tone. "All that's left of our house is the cellar foundation and the front steps."

"What about that rope around the chimney?" asked Sally.

Tommy looked at her in disgust. "A little old rope like that couldn't hold a big house like ours." He looked at Sally again. "Did your house go?" he asked.

Sally suddenly came to her senses. "Well—no," she said. "Ours is still standing."

The others all stared at her, as if having a house was something to be ashamed of. Tommy Dillon looked down his nose at her. "Just water damage, and the house didn't go?" he asked.

"Yes," said Sally.

"Well, you didn't feel nothin' then," he said flatly.

"We had to get out in a boat," said Sally feebly.

"Huh! That's nothin'," said Tommy. "What I want to know is, did you lose every single thing you got? Your bike and all?"

"No," said Sally, "we still got our beds upstairs and . . ."

"Well," said Tommy emphatically, "you don't know much about a flood then."

Sally wanted to protest, but could not. Barbara, who had only had water in her cellar, had said nothing, had just listened.

Values were twisted, somehow. Instead of a tragedy, losing one's home had become something to be proud of. As with the adults, so it was with the children. The people who lost everything became heroes and achieved prestige. They would hardly speak to those who still had homes, even though those homes had been badly damaged.

The children began to boast of their losses.

"We lost two bikes," said Jerry Nelson, "mine and my sister's."

"My mother lost her marriage ring," said Carol Rosansky. "She kept it in the top drawer of her bureau in a jewelry box. The whole bureau went."

"Our mother lost her Bible and her wedding picture and her

cedar chest," said Ray Marberry, who had come up.

"And our daddy lost his projector that cost a hundred dollars," said Ray's brother Ralph.

"Huh!" said Tommy Dillon. "That's nothin'. We lost everything we ever had except the clothes on our backs. And our whole family—all nine of us—were rescued by a *helicopter!*"

It was Barbara Boyd who had the courage to speak up.

"You're not the only one, Tommy Dillon," she said. "My daddy said over ninety families in this town alone lost their homes and everything."

"Is that *so!*" said Tommy.

Barbara turned to David Joruska. "Where are you living now, David?"

"At Lakewood Acres," said David.

"Where's that?" asked Sally.

"Over at West Hartford," said David.

Tommy turned on David. "Are you living in that old Army barracks project?" he asked. "There's not even a decent sewer there, and you have to pay $48 a month. In winter you freeze and in summer you bake."

David said quietly, "It's better'n nothing. All my friends are over there—all the River Bend kids. They're going to send a bus to bring us back to our own school, as soon as school starts." David paused, then went on, "The only thing I don't like about it, my dog died of distemper there. He drank some flood water. That first night after we got there, they told me my dog was dead. My father and mother were sorry too. They liked him. I carried him out in my arms."

Nobody said anything. *We still have Rusty,* thought Sally, remembering how the dog had jumped to the window sill when they were getting out.

David turned to Tommy, "Where *you* living now, Tommy?"

Sally wanted to know too. "You went to Vermont to your grandfather's, didn't you, Tommy?"

"We never got there," said Tommy in a low voice. "Couldn't make it—all the roads was washed out."

"Where did you go then?" asked Barbara.

"The Army men never stopped at Red Brick Road to let us off the duck, like they said they would," answered Tommy. "They took us clear over to that school and then to that crazy barracks project where David lives. My Dad didn't like it there, so some friends of his found us a Girl Scout cabin to stay in. It's cold there, though, at night. It's right in the dark damp woods and there's no stove. So we're just *camping.*" He stopped for a minute, then went on bravely, "We're gonna be living in a trailer by Monday. The Red Cross promised us one. A big six-person trailer for all nine of us."

"That's nice," said Barbara. "I'm so glad."

"Do you think you'll like it, Tommy?" asked Sally.

"Like it?" said Tommy. "Heck, no! It's too little. We'll bump each other. We'll knock things down. But what do I care?"

"Where are *you* living, Carol?" asked Barbara.

"With some strange people I never saw before," said Carol, "up in the high part of town. They're all right, but—"

"Don't you like it?" asked Sally.

"I was lonesome for my mother," said Carol. "I cried because she stayed far away on the other side of town."

Sally thought of all her schoolmates whose homes had been washed away. Now they were living in temporary housing, or with friends or with strangers—the children separated from parents in many cases. The real impact of the flood reached Sally and filled her with sadness.

Suddenly into her mind popped the image of her shiny gold compact, the compact that Tommy Dillon had taken from her so long ago. It had seemed so important then, but now had lost all meaning. Somehow she must let Tommy know. And mixed up with her desire to tell him, was a deep sympathy for all he had suffered.

"Remember that compact you took, Tommy?" she asked.

Tommy hung his head. All his bravado was gone. "I'll buy you a new one. I'll get some money—some day."

"No," said Sally sharply. *"Don't do that!* I don't ever want to see one again."

8

CLEAN-UP TIME

Do we have to have another shot?" asked Sally. "I don't want to get sick again."

"You'll be a lot sicker if you don't get them," said Mrs. Graham. "Everybody needs three shots. It takes two weeks, spacing them a week apart. We all have to have them before we can go back."

"When are we going?" asked Sally excitedly.

"Not till the house is cleaned up," said Mrs. Graham.

Mr. Graham had obtained a pass. So he and his wife had paid

their first visit to the flooded house. When they returned, they were very blue.

"The front yard is full of junk," said Mr. Graham. "There's a gulley five feet deep washed out by our front porch. Perry Wilson's truck is wrapped around the elm tree. Somebody's car is there too, upside down and filled with sand."

"Daddy put a mark up on the door frame to show how high the water came," said Mrs. Graham. "Perry Wilson pulled our gutter down, trying to climb up on our roof. Later he took off his shoes and swam the swift current to the elm tree. He hung there for thirteen hours till a helicopter picked him up."

"Mr. Wilson in our tree?" asked Sally.

"Yes," said Daddy, "and another man in the apple tree in the back yard. Both were saved."

"Most of the back yard is washed away," said Mrs. Graham. "The river bed has come almost up to the house. Vegetables and flowers are gone. It's all just sand."

"What about the lawn chairs that we put on the back porch?" asked Bobby. "And Rusty's doghouse? Are the bikes still there?"

"I saw one chair hanging up in a tree." Daddy laughed. "The others are buried in the sand. So are your bikes and the doghouse. I didn't see them anywhere."

"And so are most of my pots and pans," added Mother, "and all our shovels and tools and a lot of our clothes. I was ironing the day before Flood Friday."

"Guess what I found up in the apple tree?" asked Daddy. "Two bedspreads, a shirt of Bobby's, a dress of Sally's, an apron of Mother's and Tim's little red wagon."

The children laughed.

"My sewing machine is buried out there in the sand too," said Mother. "But I found my earrings still on the window sill in the kitchen. The water was up almost to the top of the window, but they were not washed away."

"Goody, goody!" cried Karen. "Mother has her earrings!"

"Did you go inside the house?" asked Bobby.

"Not very far," said Mother. "Daddy knocked down the door to get in. It's a sea of mud—horrible. The piano's falling apart."

"Under the mud, the floor boards are swollen and lifted," said Daddy. "The icebox and electric stove are ruined. Maybe I can get the motor on the washing machine baked—I don't know."

"We saw only one thing to laugh at—Bobby's sign!" said Mother. "That gave us courage. NOBODY HOME BUT WE'LL BE BACK!"

All this time Mrs. Boyd and Barbara had been listening.

"I'll come and help clean up," said Mrs. Boyd.

"We'll all go," cried the children.

Mrs. Graham shook her head.

"But I can help, Mother," said Sally. "I can scrub floors."

"And I can shovel out mud," said Bobby.

"I never knew you so anxious to help before," said Mrs. Graham. "But you must wait till the house is cleaned. It's too much of a health hazard. Children are ordered to keep out."

"The fire department has run a water pipe down the street now," said Mr. Graham, "so we can get water."

"Good," said Mrs. Boyd. "So many people were trying to clean mud out without a drop of water."

"The prisoners from Wethersfield are shoveling out people's cellars," added Mr. Graham, "and the Army bulldozers are shoveling up fallen trees and wrecked cars. It's wonderful how the whole country has sent help—trucks, bulldozers, men, food and clothing."

Two days later, Mrs. Graham waded into the front yard of her home, loaded down with shovels, brooms, mops and pails. To her surprise, she saw that the worst of the mud had been shoveled out.

"Somebody's been here, working," she exclaimed. "The Wilsons, I bet."

She went from one room to the other. She had to walk care-

fully, for the mud was slick.

"Well! Looky here!" She opened the refrigerator door, then slammed it shut. "Phew!" she cried. "Everything rotten in there." She called her husband. "It doesn't look like the home we left, does it, Robert?"

"It will when we get through, though, Carrie," said Mr. Graham.

"Well!" said Mrs. Graham, whipping off her scarf and coat. "No time like the present. Let's get to work. Good thing it's turned cool. Question is just what to do first."

"Shovels first, then brooms, mops, and water last," said Mr. Graham, on his way down cellar.

Soon shovel and broom were swishing out the floor. To keep her spirits up, Mrs. Graham started to sing:

" 'Home, home, sweet sweet home,
        Be it ever so humble,
        There's no place like home!' "

"Hi, there! Hello!" called a cheery voice.

"Is that you, Elsie?" answered Mrs. Graham.

Mrs. Perry Wilson came in. Looking around, she exclaimed, " 'No place like home'—you're right, Carrie. After this, we'll appreciate our homes as we never did before. But you and I seem to be mighty dirty housekeepers, don't we?"

The women fell into each other's arms and laughed until they cried. Mrs. Wilson told again of her husband's ordeal and rescue.

"I've shoveled two wheelbarrows of mud out of the downstairs bathroom alone," said Mrs. Graham.

"We didn't get that far," said Mrs. Wilson.

"I just knew you folks had been here," said Mrs. Graham. "Haven't you any mud of your own that you come over here hunting more? There's nothing like having good friends."

"Hey, you two up there!" called Mr. Graham from the cellar. "Want some night crawlers? The cellar's full of 'em. And here's a live turtle for the kids!"

"What next!" The women laughed.

That night the children were surprised to get a turtle for a pet. Bobby put it in a box and they all took turns caring for it and playing with it.

As soon as the worst of the mud was out, Mr. and Mrs. Graham moved into the upstairs and slept there nights. The downstairs doors and windows could not be closed or locked, and there was danger of looters. Even though the children begged to return, they had to stay on at the Boyds.

As time went on, more and more things were salvaged. Mrs. Graham's good dishes, packed in a box, were dug out of the sand. There was not a crack or a chip on a single piece. The ironing board, the portable radio and a photograph album were found. Bobby's bike turned up, bent and misshapen, but possible to be repaired. Sally's was never found.

"Are we never going back home again?" asked Karen one day.

"Never is a long time," said Mother.

"Can't we just come and look at the house, to see if it is still there?" begged Sally.

"It's there, all right," said Mrs. Graham. "And tomorrow we have a surprise for you. *We are taking you home again!*"

"Hooray! Hooray!" cried the children, dancing a jig.

The day came at last and with it, the grand surprise.

The children could not be held back—they rushed into the house. The downstairs was clean, the mud was gone, old furniture had been repaired and some new pieces added. The new stove, refrigerator and dinette set had come from the Red Cross. Mother cooked the first meal on the new stove, and the Grahams sat down to eat with grateful hearts.

On the living room mantel there stood Mother's two antique vases.

"One of them never moved," said Mrs. Graham. "The other one fell to the floor, but did not break. I treasure them, they were my grandmother's."

The pictures still hung on the wall above the water line. They

helped to make it look homelike, though all the curtains and rugs were gone and the floorboards were still swollen and warped. The children never noticed the water stains on the walls. Besides, Daddy brought home a roll of wallpaper samples, and they all had fun choosing the new papers to put on.

The upstairs was just the same as before the family's hasty escape through the front window. Karen found her doll's bed still standing under the side window where she had left it. She put the doll in it for a good sleep. It was the first time the doll had left her arms since Flood Friday.

One Sunday in October, the Boyds came over for dinner and spent the afternoon. It was a grand reunion for both families. Mrs. Boyd was amazed at the change.

Looking around, she said, "No one could guess this house had been through a major flood. It looks just as it did before." She paused a moment. "What an experience it was! It taught us so many things."

Mrs. Graham put her arm in Mrs. Boyd's. "It was a real challenge," she said, "a test to see what we are made of. Some of us fell short."

"I don't think so," said Mrs. Boyd.

"It was a test of friendship, too," Mrs. Graham said. "How can I thank you, Alice, for keeping the eight of us for so long?"

"We enjoyed having you," said Mrs. Boyd. "It was the least we could do to help."

"A disaster like this brings out all the good in people, doesn't it?" said Mrs. Graham.

"Everybody helped," said Mrs. Boyd. "That is what made it a memorable experience."

Barbara and Sally and Karen and their mothers came out in the yard. Sally stopped suddenly and looked.

"Oh! Our Christmas tree pine is gone!" she cried. "I watched the water go up over the tip. Where will Daddy hang the colored lights for Christmas?"

"We'll plant another pine tree," said Mrs. Graham.

They walked round the house to the back yard. All the trash and debris had been carried away and the yard had been refilled with soil. The apple tree was still there, with the long clothesline attached.

"Our asparagus has come up—in October!" Mrs. Graham laughed. "We could make a cutting if we wanted to."

"And there, look!" cried Sally. "The apple tree is in bloom!"

A branch hung low with pink and white blossoms on it. Karen ran to the corner where the piles of lumber had been removed. There on the ground were violets in bloom. She began to pick them.

"Violets!" cried Mrs. Graham. "We never had any here before. The flood waters brought them."

"I'm glad they brought something good," said Mrs. Boyd. "Nature heals her wounds quickly."

"Violets and apple blossoms!" said Mrs. Graham softly. "It's a second spring—in October."

"It's like 'the rainbow set in the clouds' at Ararat!" said Mrs. Boyd. "A promise of good to come."

They stood still for a moment and listened to a chickadee singing in the apple tree.